P9-DWD-580

The Garden Monster

Patricia Reilly Giff
ILLUSTRATED BY **Diane Palmisciano**

ORCHARD BOOKS • NEW YORK
AN IMPRINT OF SCHOLASTIC INC.

To Bill, Caitie, and Conor, with love—P.R.G.

For my Aunt Dot—D.V.P.

Text copyright © 2014 by Patricia Reilly Giff
Illustrations copyright © 2014 by Diane Palmisciano

Library of Congress Cataloging-in-Publication Data
Giff, Patricia Reilly.
The garden monster / by Patricia Reilly Giff ; illustrated by Diane Palmisciano. — 1st ed.   p. cm. —
(Fiercely and friends)
Summary: Jim and Jilli plant their vegetable garden with some assistance from their dog Fiercely—but one
unidentified seed is growing into a monster plant.
ISBN 978-0-545-24460-2 (paper over boards : alk. paper) — ISBN 978-0-545-43379-2 (jacketed library binding :
alk. paper) 1. Dogs—Juvenile fiction. 2. Gardening—Juvenile fiction. 3. Plants—Juvenile fiction. [1. Dogs—
Fiction. 2. Gardening—Fiction. 3. Plants—Fiction.] I. Palmisciano, Diane, ill. II. Title. PZ7.G3626Gar 2013
813.54—dc23   2012015716

10 9 8 7 6 5 4 3 2 1   14 15 16 17 18

Printed in Malaysia   108
Reinforced Binding for Library Use
First edition, January 2014

The display type was set in P22Parrish Roman. The text was set in Garamond Premier Pro.
The art was created using oil pastels.
Book design by Chelsea C. Donaldson

CONTENTS

Time to Plant

Pom! Pom! Pom!

What was that? Was it thunder?

Whew! It was only Jim playing his drum.

"No more snow, Jilli," he shouted.

"It's time to plant!"

"Let's go, Fiercely," I said.

But Fiercely was busy.

Fiercely's paws were on the table.

He was trying to eat the seeds

Nana had bought for us. That dog!

We took the seeds out to the garden.

"I hope they grow," I said.

"Right now they look like dots and specks."

Jim held up a big striped one.

"All except for this one," he said.

We dug tiny holes and dropped them in.

Even the striped one.

Fiercely came to help.

He dug a hole, too.

He rolled around in it.

It was hard working in the garden.
But I thought of the Vegetable Parade
at the end of the summer. We'd march.
We'd dress up as vegetables.
There'd be medals that said:

"We have to watch out for bugs and slugs,"
said Jim. He leaned forward.
"I just read a book about a garden monster.
It grew huge monster plants — and ate them."
"EEK!" I said. "I hope it doesn't eat people."
"Or dogs," said Jim.

9

We watered our seeds.
Fiercely wanted to water, too.
He raced under the hose.
He ran over the garden.
He shook himself off.
Swish-splash-swish!

The dots and specks were wet.
We were wet.
And Fiercely was soaked
from his head to his skinny tail.

We looked at our garden.

"We'll get that medal," Jim said. "If only
those bugs and slugs stay away."

"And the garden monster that eats plants!"
I said.

Trouble

We counted the days.

Two.

Four.

Eight.

And all the days
that came next.
Our garden was growing!
Tiny green strings popped up
with tiny shiny leaves.

One day, we saw a fat green stem
in the middle of the garden.
It had a HUGE leaf.
"What's that?" I asked.
Jim shrugged his shoulders.
He looked nervous.
"Uh-oh," I said.

Another night, I looked out the window.
The moon peeked from behind the clouds.
Then I saw a big shadow
creeping around in our garden.
Was it the monster who grew
huge plants — like the one in Jim's book?

I jumped back into bed.

I pulled the covers up over my head.

"Help, Fiercely!" I whispered.

But Fiercely didn't come.

The next morning, Jim arrived.
I told him about the monster.
We crept out slowly to look at our plants.
We were ready to run if we had to.

The plant in the middle was
growing fast.
Now it had two gigantic leaves.
One leaf was half eaten.

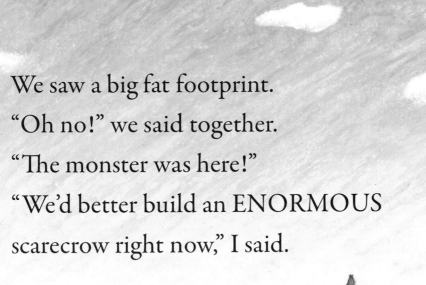

We saw a big fat footprint.
"Oh no!" we said together.
"The monster was here!"
"We'd better build an ENORMOUS
scarecrow right now," I said.

We ran into the shed.

We stuffed pants and a shirt with straw.

We gave our scarecrow a great tin-can head.

"This will scare away the monster for sure,"
I said.

"*Grrrr,*" said Fiercely.

The Garden Monster

We counted more days.

Fifty.

Eighty.

One hundred.

Soon it would be time
for the parade.
And maybe the medal, too.

Everything grew.

Juicy red tomatoes.

Bright green lettuce.

The monster's plant was in the middle.

It was high over our heads.

The stem was thick and rough.

One more leaf had been chewed.

That monster!

One dark night at bedtime,
I peeked out the window again.
The monster's plant was huge.
It had a big head and long arms.
Then I saw that monster's shadow.
He was hiding behind his plant!

24

"Fiercely," I called. "Help! Please!"
But that dog never listened.
There was just one thing to do.
I'd have to chase the garden monster myself.
I raced out past Nana.
"Save me if I need you," I told her.

I tore across the yard.

"Grrrr," I shouted.

I crawled through the garden.

I was face-to-face with the garden monster.

He had a furry face.

He had a long, skinny tail.

"Woof!" the garden monster said.

"Is that you, Fiercely?" I asked.

In the morning, I told Jim
I had caught the garden monster!
But he wasn't a monster at all!
It was just Fiercely guarding our plants!
"But what about the monster's plant?"
Jim asked.

Jim and I tiptoed through the garden.
Now the monster's plant had become . . .

. . . a HUGE yellow sunflower!
(And a tiny bug was tasting its leaf!)

The Vegetable Parade

At last it was Vegetable Parade day!

I was dressed as a carrot.

Fiercely's scarf was as green as lettuce.

And Jim was dressed as a tomato.

We pulled the wagon into the garden.

Snip-snip-snip.
We gathered in
the tomatoes.

Snap-snap-snap.
We tossed in the lettuce.

Saw-saw-saw.

We put the sunflower on top.

We joined the parade.
Our teacher, Ms. Berry,
had corn and broccoli.
Burt and his cat, Mimi, had catnip and kale.
Sarah, from the seed shop,
had onions and squash.

We began to march.

Pom! Pom! Pom! went Jim's drum.

"*Meow! Meow!*" went Burt's cat.

"*Ruff! Ruff!*" went Fiercely.

We marched down Front Street
to the Big Red Schoolhouse.
It was time for the medals.

I held my breath. Jim held his.

Fiercely nibbled Ms. Berry's broccoli.

Ms. Berry handed out medals to everyone.

"And here's a medal for Jilli and Jim,"
she said.

"Good work."

"Great growing," said Burt.

"Love those vegetables,"
said Sarah from the seed shop.

Everyone agreed that the sunflower
from our garden was the biggest plant
in the parade.
Maybe even the world!
"We did it!" we said.
Jim and I took the medal.

We didn't keep it, though.

Instead, we gave it to Fiercely.

Every night, he'd guarded our vegetables

from bugs and slugs,

and maybe even a monster!

"Way to grow, Fiercely!" we said.

"Ruff!" Fiercely answered.